A Place to Call Home

Alexis Deacon *illustrated by* Viviane Schwarz

WALKER BOOKS

AND SUBSIDIARIES

LONDON • BOSTON • SYDNEY • AUCKLAND

What is this?

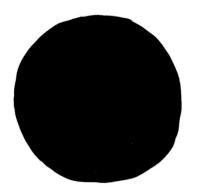

It is a small dark hole.

It is also a home.
A nice, warm, safe home.

The
trouble
is, if you
grow up
in a small
dark hole,

even
if
you
start
out
tiny,

there
comes a
time when
you've
grown
too big

and
then
you
have
to
go ...

out into the world.

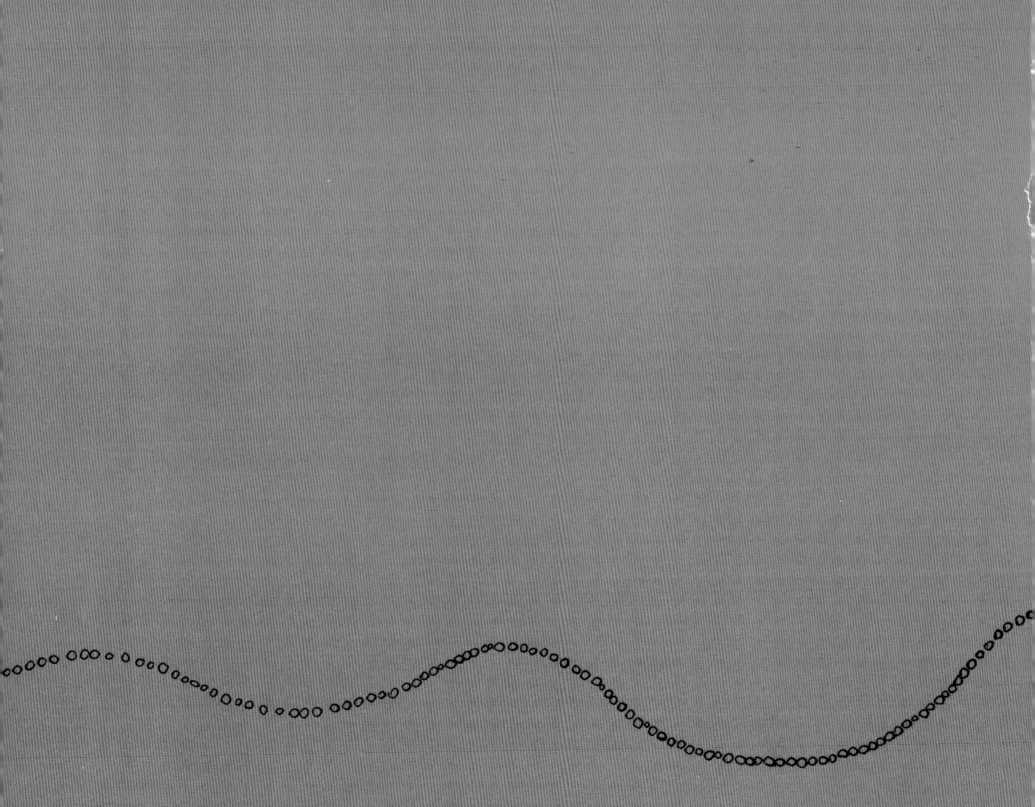

What is this?

It is big,
it is bright,
it is the whole world ...

and it is home.

For Alice, my sister ~ A.D.

For my sisters, Ina and Silke ~ V.S.

First published 2011 by Walker Books Ltd, 87 Vauxhall Walk, London SE11 5HJ

2 4 6 8 10 9 7 5 3 1

Text © 2011 Alexis Deacon • Illustrations © 2011 Viviane Schwarz

The right of Alexis Deacon and Viviane Schwarz to be identified as author and illustrator respectively of this work
has been asserted by them in accordance with the Copyright, Designs and Patents Act 1988

This book has been typeset in Stempel Schneidler

Printed in China

British Library Cataloguing in Publication Data: a catalogue record for this book is available from the British Library.

ISBN 978-1-4063-2302-3

www.walker.co.uk